Loving Hands

Tony Johnston

illustrated by Amy June Bates

CANDLEWICK PRESS

A child is born one winter day.
His mother calls him Lamb.
She hums a tune that has no words
and holds her baby's hand.

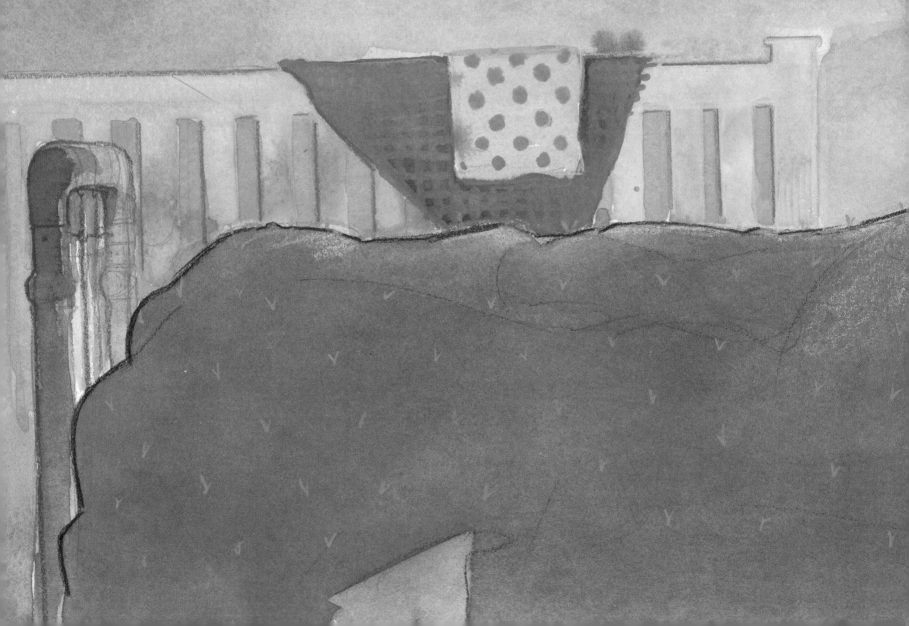

The baby wakes. The baby sleeps.
And grows. One day he stands.
He falters like a wobbly colt.
His mother holds his hands.

The baby sleeps. The baby wakes.
He claps, again, again,
for hot cross buns. He pat-a-cakes
just like a baker's man.

He likes to climb up stairs, but bears
await in shadowland.
His mother says, "We're brave as bears!"
They climb up hand in hand.

The child becomes a little boy.

He jumps and skips and runs.

And when he stumbles, when he falls,

his mother bathes his hands.

They plant a yellow sunflower row,
far taller than a man.
They pick tomatoes round and red,
the bounty of the land.

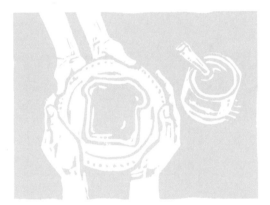

The kitchen's where they make their bread.

The warm dough swells in pans.

They bake a brown and lovely loaf,

then taste some glazed with jam.

The land's asleep. They tiptoe forth
beneath the moon, old friend.
They give new names to falling stars—
"Bright Swan" and "Gillisand."

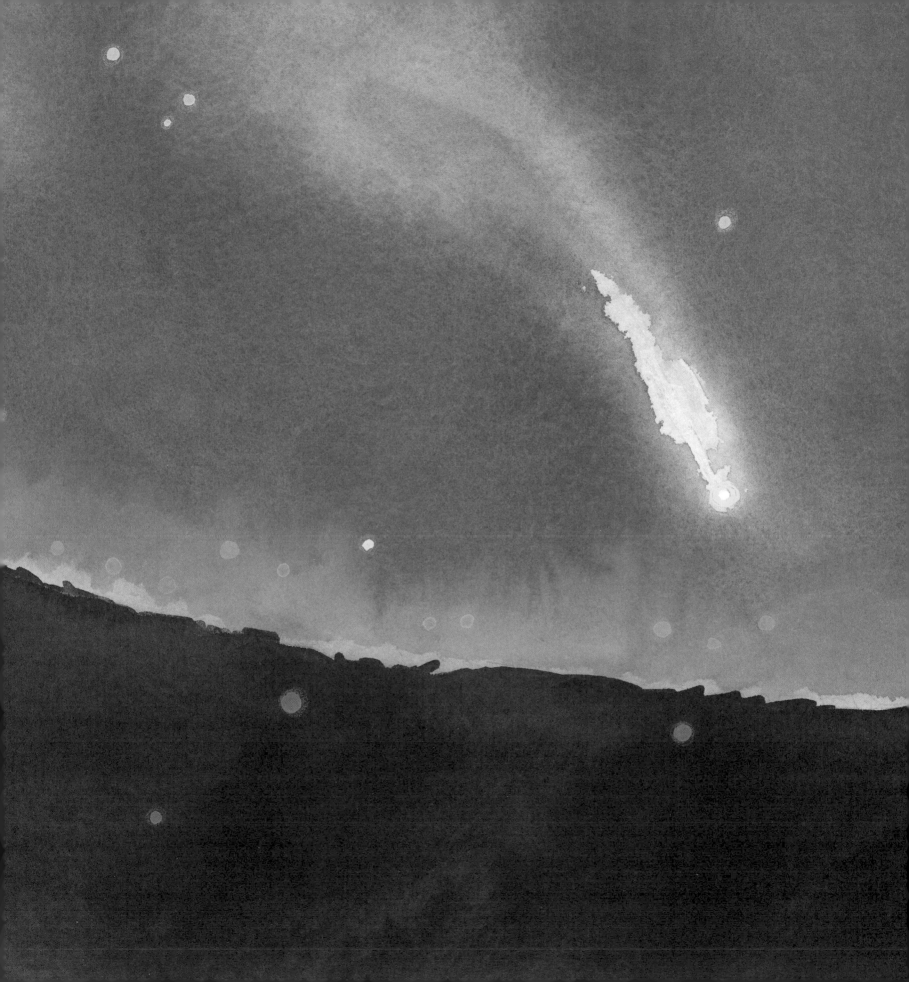

The boy is going off to school.

He asks, "Will I have friends?"

"Of course you will," his mother says.

They walk there holding hands.

He learns the letters of his name.
He writes them big and grand.
He crosses streets now on his own,
no longer holding hands.

When it is snowing, they go out.
They carry seeds in cans.
Soon winter birds all flutter down
to feast right from their hands.

The boy is grown. He leaves and waves.
"I'll visit when I can."
His mother says a prayer for him
and whispers, "Fare well, Lamb."

His mother's hair turns white as salt.
Her memories slip like sand,
except for one, dearest of all—
the memory of her Lamb.

The boy — a grown man — goes his way.
He sees her now and then.
And one day he comes home and stays,
sweet home where he began.

They sit together side by side
and watch the summer end.
He hums a tune that has no words
and holds his mother's hand.

For Margaret Taylor Johnston and her boys—
Roger, David, Jim
T. J.

For my three kids, each little hand and each little winger (finger)
A. J. B.

First edition 2018

Library of Congress Catalog Card Number pending
ISBN 978-0-7636-7993-4

18 19 20 21 22 23 CCP 10 9 8 7 6 5 4 3 2 1

Printed in Shenzhen, Guangdong, China

This book was typeset in ITC Usherwood.
The illustrations were done in
watercolor, gouache, and pencil.

Candlewick Press
99 Dover Street
Somerville, Massachusetts 02144

visit us at www.candlewick.com